America Under Neo-Nazi Occupation

America Under Neo-Nazi Occupation

Dylan Clearfield

G. Stempien Publishing Company

CONTENTS

Donald Trump Seizes Power Again
A Cynical View of America's Dire Future
BY
Dylan Clearfield

ISBN 978-0-930472-62-7
G. Stempien Publishing Company

Do not expect history
to save the future, because
history is ALWAYS written by the
victor.

INTRODUCTION

While this story is fiction, it is based on high probability when taking into account the past (Trump's first term) and the future that a new rule portends. So, this is termed a future historical fiction. This is an unbiased approach, but the cruelty and hatred that is the baseline by which the Trump first Regime operated must color the result (but only white if by Trump's preference). The American society in this essay is a depiction based on the logical progression of the beliefs and goals that is portrayed by DJT and his followers. What evolves is the ultimate and necessary identity of a country based on the ideals professed by these people and legalized by Trump's dynastic successors. It is assumed that Donald Trump and his followers will regain control of the country and install a dynasty run by DJT's descendants and, much like in ancient Rome, some of them may be raised to godhood.

1 The Stolen House

Jeff entered the vacant house accompanied by his employee-in-training, Vince. This was the residence of one of Jeff's best clients, Donald T. Donaldson. Jeff hadn't been able to contact his client for 3 weeks and decided that it was time for a visit. He was glad he dropped by.

The house had been completely emptied - completely except for the pictures hanging on the walls. They were all pictures of the founder of the current regime - Donald Trump. By law, there had to be one in each major room; a major room being any that measured larger than 8 feet by 8 feet. This room had 4 pictures of DJT and it was only 10 ft. by 10 ft.

"They moved out fucking sudden, huh?" asked Vince, a tall, skinny young man of 22, speaking in the normal expletive ripe vernacular of the day. This effect on the language was one of the holdovers from the original Trump regime and had become normalized for both genders. Jeff chose not to follow this mode of speech.

"Do you really think that's what this is?" replied his more knowledgeable associate who stood in the middle of the living room with hands on hips.

"Well, what the hell else?"

"He's a client of mine who had his homeowner's insurance all paid up 3 years in advance and a couple weeks ago had asked for money to make improvements."

"So, why the hell would he just suddenly move out?"

"That's right? Did he just move out?" asked Jeff.

"But...but he ain't the type to break the law." Vince waved his hand freely in the air. "I mean, look at all the damn pictures of the Great Trump on the walls."

"And probably all of them are the required size and the required height from the floor," noted the 41 year-old master insurance salesman and skeet shooter. "But bad things happen and even a good citizen can break the law sometimes without even knowing it."

"I can't buy that," said Vince. "He's not the kind of guy that this shit just happens to. I mean, he had a family."

"Most of them have families." Jeff tapped his co-worker on the arm and said as he headed toward the kitchen, "Let me give you a tour."

They walked into the empty kitchen. Not an appliance remained. The entire room had been cleared out - bare!

"What do you see?" asked Jeff.

"Well...nothing. Fucking empty. So?"

"I've seen this before. Nothing left. Tell me, when a person moves does he usually take his stove with him?

"Not usually," said Vince.

"His refrigerator?"

"Uh...no."

"Dishwasher or any other major appliance?"

"I ain't never known anyone to take any of those goddamned things with him when he moves," replied Vince.

"So I guess the Donaldsons didn't just move. They were moved out - confiscated."

"But, still, the family would be here. Isn't that the fucking point of furniture confiscation? Leave them in an empty house for as long as their damn sentence runs?"

"Yeah, they can't replace the furniture or get any outside help and still have to live here. But there isn't any sign that anyone is living here - bedding on the floor, empty food packages from the store. You know."

They were abruptly disturbed by the front door opening. Two men wearing white overalls and each of them carrying a long, thin rod walked into the front room. Emblazoned on the front of their uniforms was a large M and a T in red - Measurement Team

"Here to take the measurements," the taller of the 2 said.

"I'm the insurance adjuster," said Jeff walking over to them, Vince following. "Looks like you've got a lot of work to do here."

"Ah, it ain't so hard with these suckers," the man replied, shaking the rod he held.

It was an automatic measuring rod, known as the Rod of True Measurement. To measure height from the floor to the bottom of a picture frame, all that was required was to draw the rod from the floor up to the bottom of the picture and the measurement would register on the device's screen that was embedded in its side. To measure the actual size of the picture the only action required was to outline the edges of the picture with the tip of the rod and the size would be displayed.

"Seems like a waste of time measuring here," noted Jeff. "Looks like they've already been confiscated."

"We've got our orders."

"Yeah, I guess we all do," said Jeff. "Good luck."

The picture measurers got to work. Jeff led Vince to the upstairs rooms. They turned into one of the bedrooms. It was completely empty of furniture. Vince looked into the small closet which had a picture identified as DJT (Donald J. Trump) on the wall. The closet no longer had any clothing in it, but there was something laying in the corner. Vince leaned way over and snatched up a teddy bear. "Looks like this was the kid's room. Odd looking Teddy bear. All dressed up and with a shit face like a man's. And…it feels kinda prickly, like it has needles in it."

"Let me see that."

Vince handed Jeff the teddy bear.

"Doesn't the shit face look familiar to you?" Jeff asked.

Vince's gaze deflected from the bear to the picture on the wall, back to the bear, then to the picture on the wall. "I see, it's the Great Trump as a teddy bear. First one of these bastards I've seen. But, it's not a shit face. It's a beautiful face."

"How old are you?"

"Twenty-two."

"They quit making these about 30 years ago. It was called a Trumpy Bear. This feels more like a pin cushion."

"So, even the kids loved him."

"So they say."

"You seem skeptical.
"Can't afford to be."

"To be skeptical?" asked Vince.

"Can't afford to risk crossing the party line."

"What the fuck's that mean?"

Jeff cleared his throat. "We're in the insurance business, my friend. We don't take risks for anything."

"Risk. Are you afraid somebody's listening to us now?"

"Somebody's always listening to us," said Jeff.

"But we're alone in a closet in an empty room."

"And somewhere downstairs are those 2 guys measuring the pictures on the walls with rods that can probably also pick up voices from other rooms traveling in vibrations along those walls."

"Isn't that a little paranoid?" asked Vince.

"Paranoid of who?"

The 2 measurement takers started up the stairs, the sound of their footsteps creaking through the house.

"All right, we're finished here. You take this," Jeff told Vince, handing him back the Trumpy Bear. "The Donaldson's are gone and we have to find out what's going on here."

Jeff and Vince exited the house and resumed talking only once out on the sidewalk and were heading toward the company car parked by the curb.

"So, maybe the measuring crew was listening," said Vince. "But as long as you don't say any bad shit about the regime our ass is all right."

"Not really. And that's the problem. A person could make an innocent comment and have it be misunderstood so that he gets his furniture confiscated or worse - sent to a camp."

"Do you think that's what might've happened to the Donaldsons - a mistake?" said Vince. "They just fucked up?"

"I can't think of anything else. From all I know, Don was loyal to the regime. Even his middle name is Trump."

"Really? So is mine."

"Yeah, and 50 % of the country has that middle name."

The 2 men reached the car.

"What do we do about the Donaldsons?" asked Vince.

"Make some official inquiries. Then fill out all of the paperwork."

Holding out the Trump Bear, Vince said, "What do we do with this?"

Jeff took the bear from him and carelessly tossed it into the back seat. "It's considered a sacred object We're required to deliver it safely to the ministry of holy relics. Ironic - sacred object!" He grunted.

"What?" asked Vince.

"If I didn't know any better, I'd think this was a kind of voodoo doll."

"Shi-t-t-t."

They got into the car.

"I don't know what I'd do if I ever got confiscated," said Jeff. "I've got a wife and 2 kids in grade school."

"Glad I'm still single. I only have myself to worry about. And only myself to fuck up my own life."

Jeff started the vehicle. " KFC?"

"The colonel?If you can still find one that's open."

They drove away from the stolen house.

The Confiscation Act that so terrified Jeff referred to the removal of household furnishings in their entirety for anti-governmental activity of any type. The furniture is then either destroyed or redistributed, depending on its condition. It is NEVER returned. The victim cannot replace ANY of the furnishings for a set period of time - depending on the crime - and must live within that empty home. He cannot go to a hotel or live with a friend or relative for the duration of the penalty. No one could give him furniture or bring him food. He was forced to dine out if he wanted to eat or go to a local "soup kitchen." It was a miserable life! The lucky ones were the ones who had jobs, but they were usually fired after their employer learned of their furniture confiscation.

The disposition of the victim is determined by the severity of the infraction. The infractions ranged from listening to banned radio broadcasts, reading censored newspapers and books to any low level governmental agitation and outright organized insurrection.

2 How it got Like This

It was now the year 2075. All the past attempts to prosecute Donald J. Trump failed. Those at the forefront of these so-called "witch hunts" were jailed upon Trump's resumption of leadership and many of the high ranking officials involved in them were quickly executed, including: Nancy Pelosi, Adam Schiff, Jaimie Raskin, Benny Thompson, Liz Cheney, Mike Pence (hung by rope on a scaffold outside the Capitol), the Bidens and Clintons, and Adam Kinzinger. These, his worst enemies, were strung up by piano wires - except Pence - and slowly and painfully strangled to death which was the choice execution methods of both Donald Trump and Adolf Hitler.

Any opposition press was outlawed, Congress was dissolved - and the Capitol made into a country club for the super rich - the Supreme Court was eliminated, the Constitution was repealed and replaced by the Trumpian Declarations and DJT took absolute control of the country, moving the capital to Mar-a-Lago. He ruled by fiat and by raising temporary tribunals to do his bidding. His sons and their sons were the designated heirs to the Trump Dynasty and they would rule for the foreseeable future. There was not any opposition to confront them. In the year 2075 A.D. Eric Trump was still the reigning dictator.

Once one of the wealthiest nations in the world, the former United States, was now one of the poorest of all the major industrialized countries. Shortly after the violent takeover by the Trump Regime, the Treasury was ordered to default on paying the national debt which ruined the economy and made the dollar nearly worthless in the rest of the world. But the rich continued to get tax breaks and lived the lives of a new breed of aristocracy. The military, however, continued to be heavily funded and this allowed for a Nazish type of Anschluss first with Canada and then with Mexico so that Americans could not hope to safely expatriate to either of those countries.

Seeking to avoid its worldwide debts, like any other common deadbeat, the United States officially changed its name to Trump's New America (TNA). The country then secured a major loan from the USSR (formerly Russia) to assure tax breaks for the super wealthy by giving the state of Alaska to the revived Communist regime as collateral. The people living in that former state became Soviet citizens overnight, without warning.

Within the TNA (Trump's New America), the draconian Trumpian Declarations that were enforced by the regime were so restrictive against sexual freedom, ethnic diversity, musical tastes and any number of other social behaviors that what developed from this was a type of pseudo, false 1950ish morality and a society into which all citizens were indoctrinated. Anyone claiming LGBTQ affiliation was jailed and placed in insane asylums. Being gay was illegal and criminal.

What might seem like staid religious beliefs were in truth firm adherence to intolerance. In this way, although the White population was now a minority class, it continued to dominate the country in a mirror of the apartheid system of the Union of South Africa as it existed in the late 19th and early 20th centuries.

Donald Trump - the first king of the United States - set the moral standard for society and this was strictly maintained by those who followed in his line of succession. Many of the millions of true believers in him wore a Donald Trump tattoo on their wrists - either depicting his face or spelling out the name TRUMP.

One of the strangest of current laws was the Act of God Provision whose foundation was based on a classic enactment of mystical power by the original Donald Trump in his first term. It hailed back to an event in September 2019 when it is now believed that DJT personally changed the course of a hurricane by using a sharpie on a weather map to supernaturally redirect its route.

The prevailing myth was that due to his god-like ability he was able to control the weather, and due to this belief the Master Trump decreed the Act of God Provision; this law provided that any time an inexplicable event occurred to intervene in any legal process it automatically conferred innocence upon the accused party (unless he were Black or a Jew). The only way that a confiscation could be terminated or its guilt expunged was by invoking the Act of God Provision. This would be exculpatory if such an event occurred during the proceedings, harking back to the Master's super human abilities, conferring them on the victim of the procedure.

By law, Acts of God - must be shown to exclude any and all human causes. The intervention of Acts of God were extraordinarily rare!! In fact, none had ever been recorded in the Trump Age. The reason this odd law was so prominent in the legal system was because - like the founder of the dynasty - this was a very litigious state and it was considered a necessary element. The reason it was so important was that if a person were exonerated by an Act of God it meant that the chosen one - the Great Trump - had acted on your behalf, making you special among all men. This had yet to happen.

It is the enforcement of bizarre laws like this and the Confiscation Act that impressed a wider impact of absurdity onto a reflectively bizarre American society as a whole around which this story of the future evolves.

3 Death Files

In the 1950's a particularly insulting form of postcard aimed at women had a wide popularity. These showed a well dressed female while engaged in some errand - usually shopping - often carrying a grocery bag in one hand and a hat box in the other. She suddenly has the back hem of her skirt caught in a door of some type, causing her not only to lose her packages but also causing her panties - always pink - to drop to her ankles. There is always a man of some official type nearby - policeman, mailman, bus driver, elevator operator - who is gleefully observing the woman's dilemma, often looking as foolish as the woman, it should be noted.

It was just this type of postcard that Molly the meter maid found placed under the windshield wipers of a number of the cars she was checking for overtime that were parked on the street where Jeff and Vince pulled their car. The post cards had obviously been placed there as an unflattering message to Molly. The cards showed a meter maid's short skirt being caught on the end of a bumper, causing her to drop the ticketing device she was holding and her pink panties to drop to her ankles while a nearby letter carrier viewed the sight with great enjoyment.

Jeff parked the car near where Molly was checking meters. He owned a 2048 Rhombus, one of the older models. It had a hood, a trunk, 4 doors, 4 tires and a steering wheel. In other words, a basic car. Due to the default on the country's debt, new cars became a luxury for only the very wealthy while most other people, if they could afford any transportation at all, owned vehicles of an ancient vintage. These old wrecks were kept alive and running by constant repair when and if parts could be had.

Molly rushed upon Jeff as soon as he mounted the sidewalk from his car. She waved the insulting postcard in the air as she flew toward him.

"Look what some dumbass is leaving all over the neighborhood," she whined, forcing the card before Jeff's gaze.

Molly was a medium-sized, 20 year old who was attired in the official very short skirt and blue blazer that meter maids in this city wore.

"Look at this picture. Nothing like that's ever happened to me. It couldn't happen that way. Want to know why?"

"Why?" asked Jeff.

"Here's why! Just don't grab me between the legs, okay?"

"Sure."

Molly posed one leg high on the bumper of Jeff's car, balancing with pin-point accuracy on the pointed toe of her high heel shoe. The edge of her skirt rode up, revealing the top of her silk stockings and the clips which attached them to the straps of her garter belt. A tattoo of the face of Trump was revealed on her upper thigh.

"Do you know what else is under my skirt?" asked Molly as Vince gaped from the distance like a hyena.

"I have a good idea," said Jeff.

"But do you know how it works? How it really works?"

"I think I've got a good idea of that, too," evaded Jeff.

"No, no, no I mean how the clothing is held in place one piece over another."

"No, I never really considered it," replied Jeff.

"Sure, just like all men. Considering the amount of time men spend undressing women one would think that you would have some idea of the order in which a woman's underclothes are put in place."

"But..." Jeff stammered.

"If you would look under my skirt you would see that there isn't any way that my panties could just drop to my ankles." Molly snapped her leg back onto the sidewalk. "They are kept in place beneath the garter belt. Beneath it."

"Okay."

"Which is why this stupid postcard is giving out faulty information."

"Why are you showing, uh, telling this to me?" Jeff wanted to know.

"Because you're not like that grinning baboon of an employee of yours over there." Molly pointed toward Vince. "You understand things."

"Maybe so, but why tell me about the postcards?"

"You might have some idea who the jerk is that's spreading them around and what he hopes to accomplish."

"Have you given anybody a ticket on this block lately?" Jeff asked.

Molly's eyes bloomed with understanding. "You mean - somebody I ticketed might be trying to make me feel stupid and foolish?"

"That's right."

Molly raised her mini-computicket reader from her side so she could scan the screen for recent tickets given out. She started walking down the sidewalk as she scrolled through the list, after giving Jeff a thank you.

"Let's go, grinning baboon," Jeff said to Vince, leading him the short way to the front door of the Mutual Insurance Company's front door. Flying over the door was the Flag of Trump, a depiction of his fierce, warrior face amid a blue field and rifles. Since he was now the state, there was not the need for any other design on the flag but his face.

Jeff and Vince stood under the great flag for a moment so Vince could have a smoke before they went inside.

"You talked about being an insurance man earlier," said Vince. "Why did you first become one?"

"Not a long story there. I did all the mental computations and figured that it would be the most likely business to offer the highest return for the work I put in. So I started this company."

"Shit, man! You just said a lot of words without saying a damned thing."

"Sure, that's what a good insurance man does."

"Something I ain't learned yet."

"And on those old 1950 shows like 'Leave it to Beaver'..."

Vince sharply interrupted. "Hold it, man! You mean they once had a show on television all about a woman's pussy?"

"No, no Beaver was a kid the show was named after. But his dad was an insurance salesman. And on another tv show 'Father Knows Best' the father on that show sold insurance. So, I thought I'd try that. They seemed to have done pretty well."

"Sure, makes sense. What did you do before you became an insurance salesman?"

"I issued travel vouchers to people wanting to visit places across the country."

Vince nodded, drawing on his cigarette. "Sounds like a pretty...fancy type of job. Why'd you leave?"

"I didn't like the odds."

"The odds?"

"Well, a lot of the places people wanted to visit used to be their old hometowns or neighborhoods but were now restricted. I didn't like having to turn down so many old, miserable people who just wanted to visit their old hometown."

"I guess you can't go home anymore." Vince noted, tossing away the cigarette stub.

"Maybe."

Jeff led the way inside. This was a small streetside office with an old fashioned interior, having 3 desks and work areas by the back wall and a long couch for customers by the front window. There were 4 regulation sized pictures of the Great Trump on the walls, each one set at a cardinal directional location. The office seemed blessed with his glorious image.

The middle desk of the 3 belonged to the secretary Melanie, a business-like 43 year old who was very protective of Jeff and the company. She'd worked here since the beginning, 12 years ago, and was busy typing when they came in.

"How're you doing today, Mel?" Jeff queried.

"Seeing that nobody's come in and tried to grab me between the legs yet, I seem to be doing all right."

"Let's keep it that way."

"I saw you out there flirting with Molly," Melanie joked with Jeff. "Was she showing off the latest in women's underwear?"

"Yeah," Jeff played along, "I told her my wife Peggy was looking for some cheap lingerie."

"I can tell you all about that. Why not just ask me?"

"Are you bucking for a raise?" asked Jeff, taking a seat behind his desk to Melanie's right. "Do you need some fancier lingerie?"

"My husband might enjoy that."

"I'll have to have a talk with Sam then."

Vince quietly took his place at the desk to the left of Melanie and logged onto his computer.

"I've got a notification here," Vince called across to Jeff. "It's from the Department of Re-education. About the Donaldsons."

Jeff checked his computer. "Yeah, I've got one, too. Do you know anything about it, Mel?"

"Something about the Donaldson's son." Melanie said.

"Maybe they can tell me what happened to the rest of the Donaldsons, too," noted Jeff. "It looks like they were confiscated."

"I'll check into the Ministry of Confiscation's records for recent additions," said Melanie. "It'll take a few minutes."

While Melanie feverishly pecked out codes on her keyboard, Jeff stood up and walked over to the window, peering out onto the city street. A small, spontaneous parade of about 15 men in bright red baseball caps marched past the office, fists clenched and raised in the air, shouting, "Hail to Trump the Great one." Vince jumped up and joined Jeff. The parade continued to the end of the block, then disbanded as abruptly as it had begun.

"Maybe they're getting ready for his birthday celebration," Jeff noted.

They were called from their brief amusement by Melanie. "The Donaldson's son was sent to the Clayhammer Reduction school. That's all I have."

"I'd like to have a word with the people there."

"Why are you so interested?" Melanie asked.

"Let's just say that the affairs of a good client concern me."

Jeff went back to his desk and scraped up his keys.

"Want company?" asked Vince.

"No, this is something I have to take care of by myself."

Jeff gave a goodbye salute to Melanie, then departed.

4 Reduction School

The purpose of the state run reduction schools was to reduce the amount of learning in a student's mind so that it would leave more space for indoctrination. Thus the name - Reduction School.

Jeff drove down block after block of depressing city streets of boarded up houses and apartment buildings as well as closed down businesses. Shanties and tent homes had been raised in the yards and parking lots outside of former tenant's homes. Due to the collapse of the economy when DJT refused to pay the national debt, 45% of the entire population was made homeless and 53% jobless. In this environment, the confiscation of furniture made a type of sense, causing those who still had homes to be essentially homeless. It made these people equally hopeless and powerless, a sick joke on America by the Great Donald.

Jeff arrived at his destination. The building that he drove up to looked more like a prison than a school, surrounded by a 12 foot high chain link fence that was topped with razor wire. On guard at the front door was a uniformed, armed officer. He checked Jeff's wrists to see if he wore the Trump tattoo and when he didn't find any he only reluctantly allowed him entrance.

Jeff then found himself in a long, dimly lit and empty corridor whose walls on both sides were lined with pictures of all possible members of the Trump family.

Blooming on the back wall was the most striking sight of all. A huge mural took up the entire space, depicting Donald Trump on Mount Rushmore, placed right before the bust of George washington. This was a replica of the original photograph of the actual site.

Donald Trump's wish of being placed on Mount Rushmore with the other great presidents had been realized in his lifetime. And he stood out prominently among them, taking up more space than Washington and any of the other presidents.

The expansive mural was fully lighted 24 hours a day from all directions.

Jeff was too busy gazing at the amazing mural to immediately notice the large poster inside the door into which he almost slammed.

Witten upon the poster was the pledge of allegiance to Donald Trump, officially named : The pledge to ever Trump his name:

I pledge allegiance to Donald Trump
And to his victory on January 6th.
May his flag of might and glory
Forever wave above the land
He so bravely conquered and
Made so great again.

Strung along the very top of the walls were slogans which simply read: Never forget January 6, 2021 and, We Kept Jews From Replacing Us.

Jeff investigated down the hall when he heard singing coming from one of the indoctrination classrooms. He peeked inside and saw a class of 9 year olds, singing a special song (to the tune of the popular piece dedicated to the late Mao Tse-Tung by the Red Guard).

Trump, Trump, Trump
You give my throat a lump.
Trump, Trump, Trump
You make my heart just jump.
By your powerful gestures and
Genuine words of wisdom
You reveal why you are
The Chosen
One, One, One.

"Appropriate song, don't you think! Jeff was surprised by a booming male's voice from behind.

He spun about to face a tall, hulking, uniformed man in a black and silver uniform adorned with the oath Keeper badge prominent on the shoulders.

"The pledge is recited every morning and the song is sung 3 times a day," the headmaster in uniform told Jeff.

"Very good," said Jeff.

"So - who the fuck are you and what is your business here?"

"I'm Jeff Donner. And I'm here on official business. I'm an insurance investigator doing research on one of my clients. I was told that one of the children of one of them had been removed here."

"I see. Well, let's go into my office and see what this shit is all about."

Jeff was led into a small cell of an office that had bars on the one window and weaponry of all types attached to the walls, including maces and axes, halberds and swords. The commandant seated himself behind a heavy metal desk and Jeff took a hard, steel chair in front of it.

"No comforts here," grunted the mustached man with the grim, puggish face. "Fuck no. Not for me. Not for those little bastards either." He pointed toward the classrooms in general. "Those motherfuckers are going to learn the right way - the Trumpian way."

"Somebody's gotta teach them," Jeff played along.

"So, what the fuck are you doing here again?"

"Checking up on one of your students. Trying to find out just why he's been brought here."

"Yeah, right. What's his name?"

"Donald T. Donaldson, Jr."

"Fine sounding name. Wonder what he did."

The commandant pressed a button on an interoffice intercom, saying into it, "Miss Rundle, look up the files on one Donald T. Donaldson, Jr, will you honey?"

"Right away, sir," came the syruppy obedient response.

"What kind of kids do you have here?" asked Jeff.

"The kinds that can still be saved. None of the lower classes, the non-white, or Jews. They don't need schooling, just training to be good workers and servants. You know."

"Yes, their employers usually keep the useful ones well covered with insurance."

"That's smart. If one of the assholes hurts himself on the job, his owner can collect on his stupidity."

Soon after the Trumpians took control, a type of eugenics was put into practice. Only 10% of the non-white population was allowed to breed and their children were then placed in special state run facilities where they learned how to perform the heavier, more dangerous menial work. The non-whites of the population who were not selected to produce children for this purpose had the choice of either being sterilized or executed. Of course, children were produced illegally and this created a large criminal element. There were also many people who tried to pass as white but were not legally biologically white.

"I tell you one thing," said the commandant, "none of them bastards in this school belong to the Trump Youth." He then broadly grinned, displaying a row of greenish teeth, "Not yet anyway. I'll work on 'em, though. Make the Master proud."

"I'm sure you'll do all you can."

"Short of killing the bastards!" guffawed the commandant.

"Yes, short of...

Jeff was interrupted by Miss Rundle's reply over the intercom. "Sir, he's been transferred."

"Transferred!" said the commandant. " Where to?"

"An extermination facility I'm afraid."

"Don't be afraid!" roared the commandant. "If that's where they sent him, that's what the bastard deserves."

Jeff was usually steeled against shock, but this news did knock him off kilter. "What - did he attack and kill someone while he was here?"

"There's no record of it."

"Then why was he transferred?"

"You'll have to find that out for yourself."

The commandant then rose, signaling the end of the meeting. Jeff got up as well and headed toward the door. As he left, the commandant said to him, "You might want to check out our chapel before leaving. It's at the end of the hall. It has a good effect on our students, Might do you some good, too." The commandant then summoned his secretary, "Miss Rundle, come into my office please, I have some special close work for you."

Jeff was curious as to why the commandant directed him to the chapel. There seemed to be an underlying message in this suggestion.

Jeff walked to the end of the still empty corridor and stopped before the chapel door, staring at its simple face for a moment. Its only identifier was the word *chapel* in small white letters at eye level.

Jeff entered. The small, square room was brightly illuminated by track lighting. Glaring under the bright glare was a gold plated half-sized statuette of the original Donald J. Trump, the wave of his red hair exaggerated in its sweep. The statuette stood alone and indignant in the center of the squat altar. Emblazoned on the wall behind the altar was the sign of Trump on the cross which represented 3 of the great tribulations in life he'd faced and overcome: 2 false impeachments and 1 stolen election:

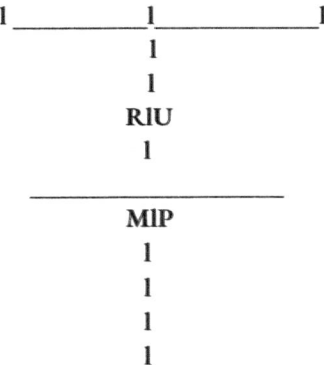

During the later years of his reign, the first Trump had much success countermanding the teachings of Jesus Christ and replacing them with his own ideology even among most theologians. Turning one's cheek to aggressors was considered a wasted act of weakness. It was replaced by the philosophy of: "Do unto your neighbor before he does unto you." This, among other beliefs, was replaced by concepts of power and the importance of defeating one's enemies instead of understanding them. And, the most important among the accepted beliefs was, "The ends justify the means."

Jeff exited the chapel. He didn't feel any more holy, but he did feel a little more anxious. It must've been all those bright lights.

This was one building that Jeff was relieved to escape.

5 Gestapo Interview

Jeff returned to the office still in a state of confusion. It didn't last long. His secretary had an important message for him.

"The Ministry of Confiscation wants to see you."

"I don't like the sound of that," said Jeff.

"I don't like the way they sounded."

"When do they want to see me?"

"Now. They're holding a spot open for you."

"Would you like to come with me?" Jeff joked.

"They said to come alone."

Vince just looked up from his desk and shrugged.

Jeff headed toward the door. Getting a summons from the Ministry of Confiscation was like getting a summons from the Gestapo. So, he was out the door again, en route to visit another governmental agency.

It was a grim drive to a grim location. The 4 story high Ministry of Confiscation's building was constructed in the classic style of the 3rd Reich, sturdy stone and functional yet symmetrically pleasing designs in form and furnishing. Dangling down the outside walls were flags of both the historic Nazi design with Swastika, alongside the flag of the Trump Regime, emblazoned with the Master's macho face. They blended together.

The Ministry of Confiscation's facilities mirrored those of Nazi Germany on the interior as well. Employees were dressed in the traditional black Gestapo uniforms which were fitted with the contemporary symbol of the Oath Keepers, Trump's version of the brown shirts. Nazi flags hung from the interior walls too, as along with those of Trump. There was not any attempt to hide affiliation with the ruthless old order, now revived.

Jeff parked directly outside in the lot provided; it was assumed that at least half of the visitors would never return to claim their vehicles. He hoped he would be one of the lucky ones who did return. After climbing the long flight of concrete stairs, Jeff entered through the huge wooden, arched door-way. He directly faced the reception desk, manned by a young Nazish woman in uniform.

"Yes?" she suspiciously asked, peering up at him.

"I'm Jeff Donner. I was told that someone here wanted to see me."

"Yes, that would be Major Hogart. I'll let him know you've finally arrived." She pressed a button on a desk control system.

It was immediately bad to know that they were expecting you by name and that they felt you'd "finally" arrived.

"He's ready for you," the Naziette said. "Go to the top of the stairs and the guard will lead you the rest of the way."

Jeff mounted the wide, carpeted stairs, admiring the dark wood of the rail-ings and carefully carved posts. Looming at the top of the steps was a gaunt, severe looking man in a captain's uniform. He checked Jeff's wrists for the Trump tattoo, then flicked his fingers, saying, "Follow me."

Jeff followed him. He was led into a wide, bright office with a large picture window giving a full view of the athletic grounds beyond. On one of the walls was a huge picture of Mount Rushmore with Trump prominently in place.

Before the picture window was a massive oaken desk and behind the desk was a more grim looking man than the one who'd led him into the office. With a flick of his hand, the guard ordered Jeff to sit in the hard, wooden chair before the desk, and Jeff sat. While all of this was very intimidating and was meant to be intimidating, Jeff was not overwhelmed by it. He was ex-perienced in dealing with authoritarian figures. The guard gave a shake of the head to the major, meaning that the visitor did not wear the Trump tattoo, then departed, leaving Jeff alone with the major.

The major peered at him across the desk with lizard eyes. They even had that slow, slithery blink to them. He was smoking a thin cigarette which was jammed into one of those holders that Nazis were wont to use in war and in 5th columnist movies of the 1940's.

"How long have you known Donaldson was a Jew!" demanded the major.

"This is the first I'm hearing of it," said Jeff, coolly.

"Is it? You're a professional. You did a thorough background check on him."

"And nothing I found led me to believe he was Jewish."

"A planned oversight on your part?" the major hissed.

"A planned deception on his part."

The major nodded. "Yes, those Jews are cunning. But so are you."

"How so?"

"Could it be that you, too, are a Jew?"

"Ha," Jeff actually laughed. "My heritage is Welsh/Austrian. I could not possibly be any more white or Aryan. Just a fact. Check it out."

The major clicked a pen up and down on the desktop. "No, I don't need to check it out. I believe you."

"Why?"

"Because of your belligerence. That's the pride of Aryan whiteness. Neither a half-white nor a half-Jew acts like that."

"Okay."

"But you could be a sympathizer. You signed Donaldson as a client, knowing he was a Jew. A Jew with lots of money."

"No, I did not know he was a Jew. And, no again, he could not have enough money to make me sympathetic."

"Are you sure?"

"Suppose I signed him up, knowing he was Jewish. I also know that you would've eventually uncovered his background. Then what happens to my commissions and the premiums he'd been paying?"

"You'd lose them," said the major, biting on his cigarette holder, making a sardonic face.

"Give me credit for being a better businessman than that. And why would I risk signing up a Jew when there are plenty of white clients available."

"No, I don't think you'd be that foolhardy."

"So, Donaldson tricked me. Like you yourself noted - they are cunning."

"Cunning as little rats, sneaking food from a gentile's pantry."

"What gave him away? How did you find out he was Jewish?"

"Ah, Mr. Donner, that's one of our little secrets."

"An informer?" Jeff tried.

"There's always someone willing to turn them in."

Jeff now turned the tables on the major. "Maybe even me - huh?"

The major was momentarily struck dumb by the thought. "Why - why, what an idea. You, the informer."

"I'm not saying it was me, just, what if it was?"

"Then that would make this interview pointless, wouldn't it?"

"I'd say so," Jeff agreed. "Can I ask you something now?"

"What?"

"What became of the Donaldsons?"

"Does it matter?"

"Not to me personally. But for my business records I need to put down something."

"I see, you are very thorough. Just note that due to an unforeseen disaster, they are no longer part of the population."

"Okay, that'll have to do."

"It was not an Act of God, however," said the major. "Not even an Act of God could have saved them in any case."

"Oh," said Jeff, "I thought if an Act of God intervened it gives an absolute pardon from heaven and proof of innocence for any activity."

"Not for a Black or a Jew."

"Oh, I see. So, there's still hope for me," Jeff awkwardly joked and immediately realized it was a very bad idea.

The major withdrew the cigarette holder from his mouth slowly and deliberately. "So, let's just hope you don't engage in any conduct that will require an Act of God to absolve you."

"Of course."

The major pressed a button on a desk console and a moment later the former guard returned.

"I am through with Mr. Donner for now," the major told the guard. "Escort him out of the building."

As Jeff stood up, the major flung his arm into the air, shouting, "Heil, the Great Trump."

"Hail Trump," Jeff reluctantly responded with a little less Nazi gusto. He then got up and followed the guard to the front door, escaping another government building but with the words, "I am through with Mr. Donner for now," echoing in his thoughts. "For now?"

After Jeff had left, the major summoned a man from the next room who'd been spying upon the interrogation. He was a regular citizen, of average appearance, much like Jeff of appearance - thin, early 40's, normal head of hair.

"Well, Mr. Wilson, is that the man?"

"Yes, that's him. He's the one I worked with at the Travel Voucher Bureau."

"Very good. We will be expecting your assistance then."

"I will be glad to do what I can."

6 MAGA Movers

It was late in the day so Jeff drove straight home from the Ministry of Confiscation instead of going to the office. But when he got to the neighborhood in which he lived he discovered an enormous moving van parked in front of the house across from him. The van consumed the length of half a city block and was as conspicuous as would be an elephant standing amid this tidy suburban neighborhood.

Emblazoned on the van's side was a huge picture of DJT, his face wide with that endearing smile while he flashed his famous thumb's up sign. Advertised in bold letters under the picture was: DONALD TRUMP III AND SONS MOVERS. Beneath this in smaller lettering: Making America Greater Again One Move at a Time. Righteously marching up and down the ramp that led into the van with furniture from the offending household was the squad of husky moving men, all in red overalls and red MAGA caps.

Right at dinner time, too. Family time. When families gather at the table to share experiences of the day.

A car drove up and parked behind the moving van. Two men got out. One man walked directly to the Wilson house and the other man - an official - proceeded to the foreman of the moving men.

Jeff heard the talk between the foreman and his supervisor. "Hey, hold off on the rest of the shit," the supervisor said.

"Why?"

"Because I fucking said so."

"All right, all right." The foreman replied between chaws of tobacco. "But we already got half the damn place cleaned out."

"Well hold off on the second half," ordered the supervisor, lighting a cigarette and then heading toward the Wilson house.

The foreman spit a gob onto the street, then went to instruct his other movers to quit their hauling.

Meanwhile, Jeff headed up the sidewalk toward his house, a modest 2 story tudor style. His wife Peggy was waiting for him outside the door. Peggy was in her mid 30's, of medium build and had her red hair fixed in a modified bouffant style. She was wearing a white cotton, sleeveless blouse and tight bermuda shorts for the warm weather of early June.

Jeff and Peggy stood out on the porch, gazing at the happenings across the street.

"How long has this been going on?" Jeff asked.

"Since about 10 this morning."

"Looks like they stopped for some reason."

"Well, come the rest of the way in. Dinner will be ready in a few minutes. Beans and franks."

They went inside and found their 2 children standing at the front picture window and excitedly gazing at the scene across the street. The girl was Pamela Sue, 14 years-old with a ponytail and short shorts attire. Her younger brother was Bobby, ten-year-old with a crew cut and torn blue jeans.

"Hey, what's so interesting?" Jeff asked, smacking his hands and walking toward his children.

They rushed over to him, falling into his light embrace.

"Do you see what's happening across the street?" Bobby cried.

"It's hard to miss it."

"What do you think they did?" Bobby queried. "Why are they getting their furniture taken away?"

"I hope that little rat of a brother of Laura's didn't squeal on her and me," said Pam. "He better have kept his mouth shut or we're in trouble."

"What!" cawed Peggy with shock, grabbing her daughter by the shoulders. "What are you talking about?"

"Well, uh, Laura has a collection of music compu-chips and...and she let me borrow a couple of them once."

"What kind of music?" Peggy asked. "The banned type?"

Pam lowered her eyes and nodded. "Yeah, the Beatles, Neil Young, Monkees, Rolling St..."

"Stop! Stop!" Peggy cried. "How could you even listen to that type of slop?"

"Did you listen to any other kind of music?" Jeff asked his daughter.

"The Zombies, Pink Floyd...

Jeff cut her off. "No, I mean like other genres. Jazz? Soul? Pop? Michael Jackson?"

"Oh, no. Laura can't even get that type."

Peggy confronted Jeff. "Do you think it's serious then?"

"No, I don't think so. If it would've been jazz or soul music then we'd have something to worry about. Anyway, confiscation is usually for some type of anti-government activity, not bad taste in music."

"What kind of anti-government activity could the Wilson's have been engaged in?" questioned Peggy.

"You can ask them yourself." said Bobby who'd gone back to looking out the window. "They're coming this way."

"What!" Peggy sprang to the window, terrified. "What do they want with us?"

"Calm down, mom," said Pam, "they're our friends - remember?"

"Friends? Friends? They used to be...used to be. But now..."

The doorbell rang. Peggy screamed. She scurried off to the kitchen. Jeff went to answer the door. He opened it to his friend, Troy Wilson, the same man who had been spying on his conversation with the major at the Ministry of Confiscation. Behind him was his wife, Shirley, a 30 year old of common appearance, carrying an uncommonly large, shiny, black patent leather purse with long, thin rope handles. Both were smoking cigarettes.

"Hi, Troy," Jeff greeted him. "Come on in. Shirley, how're you?"

"Not too well, as you might imagine," Shirley said as she slinked in through the door behind her husband.

"What's it all about?" asked Jeff, leading the two neighbors into the cozy, 50ish-style living room furnished with a fireplace, stiff davenports and crooked necked floor lamps. The kids rushed off to play.

The Wilsons sat side by side on the long davenport.

"Where's Peg?" Shirley nervously asked.

"Back in the kitchen with dinner."

"Sorry we're bothering you at supper time," Troy said, tapping his cigarette into an ashtray on a nearby magazine stand. "But we needed to talk to somebody."

Shirley positioned her oversized purse between her and her husband, sprang open the catch, pulled out a tissue, and left the top almost wide open. She was a woman who fit the role of what a wife was expected to be after marriage. Shirley had 2 children - by government regulation - and then retreated into the closed room of frigidity, while still having obligatory sex with her oblivious husband.

Peggy ventured carefully into the living room, having fortified herself with a healthy helping of prozac anti-depressants. "I...I put dinner on the back burner for now," she announced.

Peggy took her place next to her husband by the mantlepiece, asking Shirley, "Where are the kids?"

Tearing and dabbing with a tissue, Shirley told her, "They've been taken for counseling."

"Oh, I'm so sorry," replied Peggy.

Peggy didn't like the way Shirley's pea-like eyes flitted across her living room furniture like a scavenger sizing up its target.

"What made you come over here, just now?" Peggy asked to distract her.

"No reason in particular," said Shirley.

"I just thought with the movers being alone at your place you might want to stay behind and make sure they don't...don't..."

"Steal anything?" Shirley finished with a smirk. "No, they take everything. The only thing we get to keep are bathroom items and some clothes."

"No, the government doesn't want to leave any unsanitary conditions behind," added Troy.

"But it looks like they've taken a break," noted Jeff. "Are you getting a reprieve?"

"Reprieve? No, they said something about having to quit operations after 6 in the evening. It just turned 6 o'clock."

"I never heard of that before," replied Jeff, suspiciously.

"Maybe it's a new fucking policy," Troy replied.

"Ha, you don't have to tell me about policies. I'm the king of insurance policies. I've got everything in this place insured for 20 times its value - and the house. Twenty!"

"That won't do you much damn good if you ever get confiscated," noted Troy.

"I hope the test never comes."

"You never know, old buddy," Troy suggested. "You might've once done the same thing I've been charged with."

Peggy spun toward her husband in terror. "Jeff! What's he talking about?"

"I haven't any idea," he coolly replied. Jeff didn't crack under pressure, even from a guilty friend.

"You used to work with me at the bureau," said Troy. "You know what it's like handing out travel vouchers. You know about the attempted bribery that goes on."

"Yep, sure do. And I know I was smart enough to keep clear of it."

"Then why did you resign?" Troy accused.

"I could say because of annoying co-workers."

"But if you're honest you could say you resigned because the examiners were getting too close to you in their investigations."

"I have no idea what you're talking about."

"Do you remember that man who came in one day dragging a metal cylinder with him?" asked Troy.

"Yeah, he kept insisting on a travel voucher for a place called Peaceful Branch, Illinois. He wouldn't take no for an answer."

"He did get that goddamn voucher he was after. And you're the one who gave it to him."

"Troy, you're fucking out of your mind!"

"Am I? We'll see about that." Troy threw his cigarette butt into the fireplace, then yanked his wife up from the davenport with him so suddenly and sharply that her purse almost spilled its contents onto the floor. "Come on, Shirl, we don't need to waste anymore time with these assholes."

Troy and Shirley Wilson stormed out the front door. They stomped back to their house.

"What in the name of Trump was that all about!" exclaimed Peggy.

"I have an idea," replied Jeff, reaching for the fireplace tongs.

"What on earth..."

Jeff shushed his wife with a finger to his lips. Using the tongs, he dug into the fireplace - dormant during the hot summer months - and plucked out the cigarette butt that Troy had tossed into the hearth. He closely examined the butt; Peggy drew near for a closer view. The cigarette butt was in reality a tiny listening device. Peggy shrugged as if to say, "What do we do?"

Jeff put a finger to his lips again and replaced the butt in the fireplace hearth.

"I think Troy came over here to try to get himself out of his jam," said Jeff.

"What do you mean?"

"He tried to implicate me in the crooked things he's doing at the voucher bureau. Maybe he thinks that by making me look guilty of something they'd give him our stove and refrigerator after his are removed."

"That's pretty rotten," noted Peggy.

"Well, you know what they say: 'Do unto others before they can do unto you.'"

Peggy headed toward the kitchen, saying, "Dinner's ready. Let's eat."

"Good idea," said Jeff. "I'll get the kids."

It was suppertime in the Donner household. And, afterward, Jeff had a great deal of work to do in the upstairs bathroom; applying heavy lacquer to replace the tiles in the floor and performing some special handiwork beneath the sink. There was no time to lose now. But he'd had it all planned for a very long time ago.

7 Dark Reminiscence

The moving van had departed from the Wilson's home by the next morning. But, a black governmental 4 door sedan had parked outside of the Donner's house. It was just after noon and Jeff was called home from work by his wife to meet the situation. He found 2 men dressed in cheap suits walking through his house, clipboards in hand. Jeff immediately confronted them.

"So, what's this all about?"

"We're taking inventory of your possessions for potential confiscation," said man 1, Biff Bannon.

"On whose authority?" Jeff demanded.

"Head of the Ministry of Confiscation."

"On what evidence?"

"I can't tell you that shit. You'll officially be notified."

"Before confiscation begins, I hope," Jeff snorted.

"You would damn well think so, wouldn't you?"

At this point, Man 2, Ronald T. Donald, walked over to them. He summoned Jeff to follow him, and the 2 men left the other behind, walking to one of the opened first floor closets that was under the steps.

Ronald pointed into the closet at a large, 3 ft. high, silver cylinder that contained a gaseous substance and asked, "What the fuck is that?"

"A canister of some form of gaseous element. Not sure what."

"Why the hell do you have that?"

"Why do you need to know?"

"We have to take an inventory of every goddamn thing in your house to make sure that you don't illegally transport any shit off the premises prior to any confiscation."

"Oh."

"So, why the fuck do you have that thing?"

"It was left over from a sick relative. I'm...sentimental. That's all, for Trump's sake.

"All right. Shit - that's all I needed to know."

Jeff turned from Ronald to let him get on with his inventory and saw the man's partner by the fireplace, stooping over the hearth. Walking over to him, Jeff asked, "Find something interesting there?"

"No," said Biff, straightening, "just counting your logs and fireplace utensils." He then went to assist his compatriot.

Jeff noticed that the combination cigarette butt-listening device that Troy had thrown into the fireplace was now gone, obviously reclaimed by Biff. Peggy joined him there.

"What's wrong?" she asked, furiously puffing on a cigarette she'd just lit.

"The infamous cigarette butt is gone."

"What's all this really about?" Peggy asked. "What was it that Troy said about giving away illegal travel vouchers?"

"First, you have to know that I expected something like this and am prepared for it."

"Something like what?"

"The travel voucher thing. I'm counting on the stupidity of the government and just a little bit of luck and help from God to get through it."

"I don't know what you're talking about."

"You're not supposed to. And I can't talk to you about it. But you know me. Do you think that I would ever get into a situation that I hadn't completely planned for?"

Peggy shook her head.

"Okay. I think you better go check on the kids now and make sure they're okay."

"Right. They're out back, playing."

Peggy headed toward the back door, leaving clouds of smoke behind. Jeff sat down on one of the stuffed sofas and looked toward the closet. The door was still open and he gazed at the oversized oxygen canister. He reminisced back to the day he got that canister and how it happened.

The aged man stumbled up to Jeff's counter. With difficulty he dragged behind him an oversized oxygen tank on a small cart. Plugged into his wide nostrils were a pair of life saving tubes that were attached to the canister.

"I...I need a travel voucher," croaked the old man.

"For where?"

"Pleasant Branch, Illinois."

"Let me check on that," replied Jeff, tapping the keys of the computer on the ledge below the counter top. After a few moments, he replied, "There isn't any Pleasant Branch, Illinois listed but the computer shows a restricted zone when I search the name."

"Yup, that's the same area. Pleasant Branch is nearby."

"But do you know what this red area - this restricted zone - is?" asked Jeff.

"It..." he paused for a breath, "it was where I was born and where I want to die."

"I can't give you a voucher for there. They don't exist. It's a government facility."

"But I have to get there. At least to Pleasant Branch."

"Turn yourself in to the authorities. They'll be glad to send you there."

"No, no - not in the facility. I just want to go home again. To die in peace in my own home. That's in Pleasant Branch."

Jeff was touched by the man's situation. The old man only wanted to die in his hometown and in his old house. Jeff could never be described as a supporter of the current regime and he maintained a strong dislike for the concept of never being able to go home again! He decided to help the man.

Although a voucher could not be printed that allowed access to the restricted zone one could be fraudulently produced for Peaceful Branch, Illinois which as a location did not officially exist any longer. Jeff typed the necessary information into the computer and printed out a fake voucher for its recipient in the name that was given to him: I. M. Moses. He then deleted all information of the transaction...he thought.

Peaceful Branch was only 15 miles north of the office where Jeff was stationed and, since the aged man had no other way to get to his destination, Jeff decided to drive him there. He was still young, unencumbered, curious, and played the odds if he judged the probability factors to be in his favor. His fellow employee, Troy Wilson, always the conniver, watched Jeff and his customer leave with great interest.

Jeff drove Mr. Moses to the outskirts of Pleasant Branch and stopped by the population sign. But under population, the amount that had been there had been whitewashed over as had the town name.

"The last that I remember," Moses said, "the population was 705."

"Are you sure this is the right place?" Jeff asked.

Moses pointed to a huge oak tree on the right which was near a small stream. "I'm sure. That's the old oak. We all knew it and loved it. It's beside the branch of the DesPlaines River which is why the town was named Peaceful Branch."

"Looks like a nice little town."

The road led into a small, typical Illinois town that looked more like one from the 1950's. It seemed a tranquil, clean, friendly place. But now it was totally deserted and in need of restoration.

Jeff started the car slowly forward. "What happened here?" he asked.

"Have you ever heard of a place called Lidice?"

"No, I can't say that I have."

"It was a small town, too, in the Czech Republic a long time ago. It doesn't exist anymore either."

"Why?" asked Jeff.

"During the second world war it was totally destroyed by the Nazis as a repriesal for the murder of some German soldiers."

"Was that what happened here?"

Jeff stopped at the first crossroads: Main and Elm.

"I was an insurance salesman. I went out of town for the day to see a client in a nearby city. When I came back the next day it was all over. My wife, kids...everybody. Gone."

"Why!"

"You know what's funny," said Moses. "I never learned why. It was never reported. And the existence of the town was completely wiped out."

"Yeah, that's why I couldn't find it listed anywhere."

"Now I want to go home for the last time. The 3 story Victorian on the corner."

Moses removed the breathing tubes. "I can live about an hour without these," he told Jeff. "You keep the oxygen tank. And...and, listen to me, keep it somewhere safe because one day it will save you."

"An oxygen tank?"

"It will save you, son, believe me - I know."

With that, Moses struggled to get out of the car. He gave a final wave goodbye to Jeff, then simply started walking down the road.

Something wrapped Jeff on the shoulder.

"Hey, bud! Get up," said Biff, the inventory specialist. "We're done here."

"What...what?"

"We're done. Say, listen pal, I just wanted to know if you'd like to save anything special from all this junk - unofficially of course." He pinched his fingers together as in the sign of collecting extortion money.

"Like what?"

"Maybe an autographed baseball or something small. Look, when those fucking movers come through this place they leave it like a goddamn tornado hit it. Nothing's left. Some of the assholes even snip off the light cords just to be dickheads. But me and my buddy aren't like that."

"No, I see that. Can I think about it awhile? I hadn't really prepared."

"Friend, time is not what you have."

Biff was suddenly interrupted by his partner.

"I have to break in on this," said Ronald. "They want to see this guy down at the Ministry of Confiscation and they want us to take him there."

Biff reached down for him. "Okay, pal. I guess time's up."

8 Final Jeopardy

Jeff found himself back at the Ministry of Confiscation. This time, he was in a small, claustrophobic type of room with a more severe looking interrogator who was attired in field military gear.

"Good afternoon, Mr. Donner, I am chief interrogator Donald Trumpman." There wasn't anything friendly in this salutation. Coming from the man who was pacing behind his victim.

"Am I under arrest?"

"We will soon see."

"I didn't know the Donaldsons were Jewish."

"That's not why you're here. You've been brought here to discuss a little matter of an illegal travel voucher you once issued."

"I don't recall any such event."

"Oh? Your own words brand you the liar."

The interrogator marched to his iron desk and withdrew a small recording device from a top drawer. "This is the recorder the lady had in her purse." He set it next to Jeff and played part of a conversation he had with Troy just a night ago.

"You used to work with me at the bureau," spoke Troy. "You know what it's like handing out travel vouchers. You know about the attempted bribery that goes on."

"Yep, sure do. And I know I was smart enough to keep clear of it."

"Then why did you resign?" Troy accused.

"I could say because of annoying co-workers."

"But if you're honest you could say you resigned because the examiners were getting too close to you in their investigations."

"I have no idea what you're talking about."

"Do you remember that man who came in one day dragging a metal cylinder with him?" asked Troy.

"Yeah, he kept insisting on a travel voucher for a place called Peaceful Branch, Illinois. He wouldn't take no for an answer."

"He did get that goddamn voucher he was after. And you're the one who gave it to him."

"Troy, you're fucking out of your mind!"

The interrogator stopped the playback.

"Remember that conversation?"

"Yes. I didn't admit to anything."

"Actually, you did," the interrogator stated. "You gave us a location - Peaceful Branch, Illinois - which does not exist in our data system because it was eliminated. How would you have known of it if you hadn't located it on our system back then in order to issue the illegal voucher for that location?"

"So that's the information that Troy was looking for - my knowledge of Peaceful Branch."

"Oh, it could've been anything. But that's where you made your mistake."

"I hope Troy got well paid for his treachery," said Jeff.

"We promised to give him your stove and refrigerator in return for his confiscated stove and refrigerator."

"So, what happens next?" asked Jeff.

"As you know, issuing illegal travel vouchers is a major offense, but not necessarily punishable by death. In your case, the infraction is much more extreme. It's because of where the voucher would permit travel to - an active death camp."

"I had my suspicions," said Jeff, "but wasn't sure until now."

"Ironically, it's the same death camp where you'll be sent. It's actually just across the river from Pleasant Branch. Your wife will be sent to the women's prison and your children enrolled in Reduction school. However..." He paused.

"However?"

"You can be very valuable to us. Very valuable."

"How's that?"

"You're an insurance man. You visit people in their homes all the time. And they also meet with you in your office. They wouldn't suspect you."

"Suspect me of what?" Jeff asked.

"Getting information about them the way Troy got it on you."

"I don't think I could be that deceitful."

"Deceitful? You'd be a patriot, serving the glorious leader of your country. What's wrong with that?"

"The method maybe," said Jeff.

"Be realistic, man. The ends justify the means. That's one of our most sacred beliefs in this country ."

"If I do agree, will I still be confiscated?"

"Certainly. You must be. It's an outward sign of your guilt."

"What about the Wilsons? What happens to them?"

"Like I said, they'll get your refrigerator and stove, but will still be confiscated."

"Why? What was Troy's crime?"

"He knew, or at least suspected, that you'd given out an illegal voucher a long time ago. He didn't turn you in right away. He's guilty and has to pay the price."

There was a pause. The interrogator finally took his seat.

"How much time do I have to decide?" Jeff asked.

"You have to agree to my proposal by the time that confiscation is concluded."

"When will confiscation begin?" asked Jeff.

"It is ongoing as we speak."

"What!" Jeff involuntarily sprang up from his chair.

"Yes, I suggest you return home and think things over if your mind isn't made up yet. But think quickly. It usually takes only about 6 hours to clear a house. Our movers are very efficient, based on the Trump model."

9 Deadline

Jeff got home as quickly as he could. The great van was parked by the curb outside his house. The Wilsons were eagerly watching the proceedings from lawn chairs in their yard across the street. Jeff's wife and kids were huddled in the front yard, watching the righteous movers marching off with their furniture.

Peggy leapt into Jeff's arms. "Jeff, what'll we do? I'm so scared!"

The kids gathered around them.

"Do be afraid - any of you. Peggy, didn't I tell you that I was always ready for any situation?"

"Yes. But...this!"

"Let's just see. If all goes well we'll be all right. For now, you and the kids get in the car. I've got to talk to the man in charge."

Standing by the front door and directing operations was a confiscation overseer, a tall, thin man dressed in black, and wearing a white fedora hat. He was the official in charge of everything. He made sure that the gas to the house was turned off if there was any, that the electricity was turned off and that the water was also shut off. This was to avoid any accidents during the moving out period.

Jeff walked up to the man who looked condescendingly his way.

"I'm here to make sure that this operation is successfully carried through," he informed Jeff. "Every piece of furniture will be removed right down to the coat hangers unless I get the order to stop from my office."

"And the light bulb cords, too?"

"The what?"

"I heard that sometimes the movers snip off the cords attached to overhead light bulbs just to be vicious."

"That's up to them. I never check on light bulb cords when I do my walk though. So, what the fuck do you want with me, anyway?"

"I was hoping to rescue an item from inside."

"Are you kidding?"

"No, I want to save one of the Master's wall pictures."

"You really do know the law don't you?" said the overseer. "I can't legally refuse a request like that."

"There's very little that I leave to chance," said Jeff.

"Okay, go ahead. I don't see what harm you could do."

Jeff gave the man a quick salute and headed into the house, skirting around the men carrying out the remaining furniture. A 3rd mover was moving through the house, making sure everything was in order for the completion of the confiscation.

Jeff then scurried up the steps to the already cleaned out top floor bathroom and lit a cigarette which he laid precariously on the rim of the tub. He'd been planning this a long time.

Opening the doors of the vanity cabinet beneath the sink, Jeff pushed aside the pipe that led up to the sink, a pipe he'd sawed loose in preparation a day earlier. He then withdrew the hose that he'd stuffed into the pipe that led into the sink from below. This hose was attached to the oxygen canister that he'd concealed in a compartment under the floor. This let loose a powerful spray of pure oxygen which quickly engulfed the bathroom.

Jeff got up, raised one of the heavily lacquered floor tiles, made sure the bathroom window was opened a mere crack, and that the cigarette was still burning. When he left, he closed the bathroom door 3 quarters of the way shut. Jeff then hopped down the stairs and loped toward the front door, needing to hurry. But he stopped himself, remembering to snatch a picture of Trump from the wall before exiting the house so as not to draw suspicion. He left the front door wide open on his way out.

The overseer was positioned on the doorstep, awaiting Jeff's departure. The movers were done with their work.

"It's all yours," Jeff told him and then hurried part way down the sidewalk.

The overseer went into the house. He closed the door behind him. When the door shut it created a draft in the bathroom which both sucked its door shut and knocked the cigarette onto the floor. The cigarette burst into a shower of tiny sparks. These tiny sparks detonated the highly oxygenated air into a mighty explosion which blew off most of the upper floors of the house.

The front door to the house was blown outward and the overseer came tumbling after, suffering only minor cuts and bruises. No one else was injured in the monstrous explosion.

Fire trucks were quickly on the scene but the house was hungrily devoured by the vicious flames. In the end, only the foundation of cinder blocks and the basement were left. A great rectangular smoking hole in the ground was all that was left.

Jeff walked over to where the overseer was standing, and sarcastically said to him, "Well, it's a good thing you got all of my furniture out of there."

A grunt was the only response.

"What did you do to my house?" Jeff then asked him. "You were only supposed to remove the furniture, not burn the place down."

"I had nothing fucking to do with it. It was an accident."

"Oh, what kind of accident? We didn't have any gas appliances so gas wasn't left on. The electricity had been turned off so there couldn't have been an electrical fire."

The overseer then summoned one of the movers over to him.

"Say, you were the last one in the house. You did the proscribed final run through, right?"

"Hell yeah," said the mover. "So?"

"So, did you see anything out of the ordinary that could've fucking caused this?"

"Fuck no. Everything was as it should've been."

"Then what started the fire?" the overseer asked.

He shrugged. "Fuck if I know. You were the last one out of the place. Did you toss out a lit cigarette butt or something?"

"I ain't that damn stupid."

"Then I don't know." The mover walked away.

Jeff tried, "Must've been spontaneous combustion, huh?"

"Yeah, I guess."

"Do you know what that is? It's an act of God."

"No, but...no...but...." stammered the overseer.

"Then if you didn't burn the place down, I invoke the Act of God provision of the law. And, if you admit to burning down the place, you're in a lot more trouble than I am."

"Oh, shit!" The overseer pressed his ever present clipboard to his head. "Oh, shit!"

"That's right. So, it's up to you to register my request with the court. You're the ranking official here."

"I guess I'll have to. There'll have to be a hearing."

"When it's set up, you can contact me at my place of business."

"All right," said the overseer. "I have all your contact information. Fuck, this is a new one for me. I Never had a house burn down on me before."

The overseer staggered off, muttering to himself. Jeff returned to his wife and kids who'd been watching from the car. He got in the driver's seat.

"What's going on?" Peggy asked with alarm.

"I'll tell you on the way to the hotel."

"Hotel! We're not supposed to be able to stay outside our own...house."

"What house?"

"Still. The law."

"Don't worry," said Jeff. "I've got it all planned out. We're booked in a place under different names where we'll stay until the hearing."

"Hearing? What's happening?"

"I'll tell you on the way."

Jeff started the car forward, leaving everyone behind in a state of shock.

10 The Hearing

The hearing was held 10 days later after a thorough arson investigation had been made of the scene of devastation. A commission of 3 people sat behind a large desk before a small group of spectators in a small room. Among the commissioners was the Chief Controller - a fat, white male in his 50's - the assistant on his right - a fat, white male in his 50's - and the overseer of the confiscation of the Donner household. Women were not allowed to hold authoritative positions in this society.

Questions were directed at a fire forensics investigative expert who sat facing them from a small desk like those used at highschool. In the audience was Jeff and his wife as well as the 2 employees from Jeff's insurance agency.

"Let's begin," said the commissioner. "Mister investigator, did you pin-point the location of the fire?"

"It appeared to originate somewhere on the second floor."

"Could you be more specific?"

"I'm afraid not. That's the closet estimate we could make. And this was only because of eyewitness accounts."

"Did you locate any source of fuel that could have caused the fire to start?" asked the commissioner.

"No, sir. Not a trace."

"Nothing!"

"Nothing at all."

"Would you consider this unusual?"

"Highly unusual. It's as if the fire started without cause."

"Very well, then," continued the commissioner, "did you find any indication of an oxidant? Something that added to the force of the fire once it was ignited?"

"No, sir."

"None?"

"None, sir."

"Then can you speculate as to what could have supplied the energy to create the massive amount of heat that burned down the structure?"

"No, sir," said the perplexed investigator. "Other than the structure itself. But this is normal. The contents of a building supply most of the fuel in any event."

"Then, did you find the existence of any form of self-sustaining chemical that could produce an unrelenting chain reaction?"

"Nothing was found."

"So, you're telling this commission that: 1) the specific location of the origin of the fire cannot be determined; 2) a fuel source that could have ignited the fire could not be found; 3) an oxidant that would energize the fire could not be discovered; and 4) there was not any evidence of a self-sustaining chemical that would have produced a chain reaction. Is that what you are telling this commission?"

"Yes, sir."

"Then, by these parameters, a fire could not have occurred."

"That is my official finding."

"Then how do you explain what occurred?"

"Sir, the only speculation I have is that it was a matter of spontaneous generation," replied the investigator.

"An act of God, in other words - as the victim of the fire claims."

"It would seem so. Only God can produce spontaneous generation."

The commissioner turned toward the overseer of the confiscation. "Do you have anything to add?"

"The mover who made the final walk through of the structure found nothing amiss. And neither did I. The gas, electricity and water were all turned off well in advance."

"What would be your assessment of the cause of the fire?" the commissioner asked him.

After a lengthy pause, the overseer reluctantly replied, "An act of God."

At this point the assistant commissioner broke in, bending stiffly forward in his seat. "But one question has not been asked."

"What's that?" queried the commissioner.

"In regard to the cause of the fire, has there been an investigation into any possibility of human agency being involved in its creation in any way? In any way?"

The investigator replied. "Yes, sir, it was investigated and we could find no possibility or incidence of a human being as the cause of the fire in question. We even examined the idea of mental telepathy."

"Another question: records show that just before the fire, the owner of the house entered the structure. For what reason?"

"To retrieve a picture of the Great Trump from inside," said the overseer.

"And that's all he did?"

"That's all he had time to do."

"Are you sure?"

"Well, he was under surveillance," lied the overseer to protect himself.

"You should've noted that in your records."

"I thought it would be self-evident that he'd be watched."

"All right, all right. That's all I have."

There was a pause.

"Very well, are there any other questions?" asked the commissioner.

There weren't any.

The commissioner then spoke again. "There doesn't seem to be any need for discussion of this matter. I have never seen a situation like this in all of my years of evaluating suspicious fires. The facts seem clear. There was not any apparent source of the fire in question. Therefore, unless there is any opposition, I am going to recommend to the Ministry of Confiscation that the accused - Jeffrey Donner - be acquitted of all charges due to the Act of God provision and that all of his furnishings be restored and any insurance settlements on the value of his home be honored."

He waited a moment for any objections. There were none.

The commissioner pounded his gavel, declaring, "This hearing is closed."

Everyone was shocked except Jeff. How did he do it? It was something he would never divulge to anyone. But he knew that pure oxygen causes things around it to burn with intense force if any item is ignited in its vicinity, particularly a hydrocarbon based lacquer like that which he used in great quantity the day before to attach the tiles to the new bathroom floor. He also knew that the container of the oxygen would be one of the first items obliterated by the explosion, and in fact it would be pulverized and melted into atoms. He also knew that oxygen could not be traced as an oxidation agent because it would be totally consumed by the fire. Thus, Jeff had created an Act of God.

11 The Decision

One week later - after living it up in a hotel for a while - Jeff and his family were summoned to an adjustment hearing at the Ministry of Affairs. The meeting was held in a simple office like environment in the business district of town and seemed out of place with the rest of this dark and terrifying society. It was, in short, a throwback to simpler and saner times.

An Adjudicator - a fat, white man in his 50's - sat behind a large desk and read from the document that had been prepared for this situation. "Good afternoon, I am the adjudicator of your assessment for confiscation. And, no, I am not a Jew."

He was not attempting humor.

"According to the findings of the commission, by way of an Act of God you have been exonerated of all guilt pertaining to the affairs leading to the confiscation procedure waged against your household. It is my responsibility to determine how this affects the outcome of the process in its entirety."

He took a drink from his Donald Trump coffee mug.

"Since the chosen one - the Great Trump - had interceded on your behalf by this Act of God it is the decision of this office that any insurance settlement on the loss of your house be honored. Also, all of your furnishings in total will be returned to your possession at a location designated by you."

He then lit a cigarette.

Jeff spoke. "While I very much appreciate the offer, about the furniture, there are only 2 pieces that I would like returned."

"Very well. Which are the 2?"

"The stove and the refrigerator."

"I see. These had been designated for assignment to the Wilson family. But this order will be overridden and the said appliances will be returned to you."

"In that case," Jeff replied, "I would like those 2 pieces along with the remainder of my furnishings to be donated to a facility for the needy."

"That is very generous of you, Mr. Donner. May I ask the reason for such magnanimity?"

Jeff had never before heard anyone use the word magnanimity before and was shocked anyone else knew it. He answered anyway. "Being that I am an insurance adjuster, I had all my furnishings and the house itself covered for 20 times their value. I prefer to replace the older items with newer models."

"I see. Very wise. It reminds me: I need to increase my insurance coverage."

"Then I might suggest visiting my friend Vince at my old agency. I just sold the business to him."

"Thank you. I will do that."

The adjudicator turned to the next page of his document, puffing deeply on his cigarette.

"Because you have attained a special classification among the citizenry due to the intercession of the Great Trump, all travel restrictions for you have been rescinded and you are hereby granted an irrevocable travel voucher which is good for anywhere on the planet and some colonies in space."

The adjudicator tipped forward in his chair and handed Jeff a triangular shaped metallic card.

"I can go anywhere with this?" asked Jeff.

"Excepting those few off-planet restrictions - yes. It is a very rare allowance."

"Thank you. I plan to use it."

"Certainly. That was the intention of presenting you with it. It is hoped that you will use them."

What he meant was that Jeff had now become too powerful a celebrity and the government appreciated it if he would go on a long trip someplace and just disappear.

"Is there anything else?" Jeff asked.

"Nothing, except..." he stood and extended a hand, "the best wishes from this administration and Eric Trump."

Jeff stood and accepted the handshake. He then led his family to the door.

12 Escape

The settlement given Jeff on the loss of his house at 20 times its value amounted to a small fortune. He took the money and purchased with it one of the most luxurious and fully outfitted RV's available. He then stocked it with food and camping gear that would last for years.

With his wife following behind in their Rhombus, Jeff led the way in the RV to the deserted town of Peaceful Branch, Illinois, the hometown of the elderly man for whom he issued that unauthorized travel voucher.

This town officially did not exist so if the case should arise that someone sought to track down he and his family it would not be possible. It was not within the restricted death camp area, but it was close enough to it to be protected by the designation of a non-existent status.

The town had been left just as it was on the day it was evacuated so there were many good homes still left in which to settle. But, since the choice was the entire town, Jeff expected it might take years to choose the one they all liked.

The End